NO LONGER PROPERTY OF
SEATTLE PUBLIC LIBRARY

RECEIVED

AUG 12 2014

DELRIDGE LIBRARY

OLIVIA™
Loves Halloween

by Maggie Testa
illustrated by Jared Osterhold

Ready-to-Read

Simon Spotlight
New York   London   Toronto   Sydney   New Delhi

Based on the TV series OLIVIA™ as seen on Nickelodeon™

SIMON SPOTLIGHT
An imprint of Simon & Schuster Children's Publishing Division
1230 Avenue of the Americas, New York, New York 10020
OLIVIA TM Ian Falconer Ink Unlimited, Inc. and © 2014 Ian Falconer and Classic Media, LLC
All rights reserved, including the right of reproduction in whole or in part in any form.
SIMON SPOTLIGHT, READY-TO-READ, and colophon are registered trademarks of Simon & Schuster, Inc.
For information about special discounts for bulk purchases, please contact Simon & Schuster Special Sales
at 1-866-506-1949 or business@simonandschuster.com.
The Simon & Schuster Speakers Bureau can bring authors to your live event.
For more information or to book an event contact the Simon & Schuster Speakers Bureau at
1-866-248-3049 or visit our website at www.simonspeakers.com.
Manufactured in the United States of America 0714 LAK
First Edition
1 2 3 4 5 6 7 8 9 10
ISBN 978-1-4814-0462-4 (pbk)
ISBN 978-1-4814-0463-1 (hc)
ISBN 978-1-4814-0464-8 (eBook)

It is almost time for the
Halloween party at school!
Olivia and Francine help
get the classroom ready.

"Can we use red and black decorations?" asks Olivia. "Red is my favorite color!"

Francine says, "Red is not a Halloween color. We must use orange and black."

If Olivia cannot have
the perfect decorations,
she wants to find
the perfect costume.
But what should she be?

"You could be a cow," suggests Mom.

"Or a lemon!" says Dad.

"Or an astronaut,"
adds Ian, "like me!"
"I want to be different,"
says Olivia.

"I could wear my ballet costume," Olivia says. But that does not seem right either.

Why? Olivia knows!
Those costumes are not
the perfect color.
They are not red!

The next day at school,
Olivia asks Julian for help.

"I am dressing up as a musician," says Julian. "I want to be a musician when I grow up."

"What do you want to be, Olivia?"
Julian asks.

Olivia wants to be lots
of things!

"You are a really good artist," says Julian.

"That is what I will be for Halloween!" says Olivia. "An artist costume can be any color!"

Soon it is Halloween.
Olivia wears her costume
to the class party.
It is red. Perfectly red!

Francine is an artist too!
At first, Olivia is upset.

But not for long!
Olivia sees the decorations.
They are orange and black
and red, too!

"You did this for me?"
Olivia asks Francine.
"Yes," replies Francine.
"More colors are more fun!"

"And more artists are more fun too," adds Olivia. "Good minds think alike!"

After the party,
Olivia trick-or-treats.
She loves getting treats!

And she loves giving
treats too!
It is the perfect Halloween!